NORTHERN SCOTLAND

Edited By Sarah Washer

First published in Great Britain in 2017 by:

Young Writers
Coltsfoot Drive
Peterborough
PE2 9BF
Telephone: 01733 890066
Website: www.youngwriters.co.uk

FOREWORD

Welcome, Reader, to 'Crazy Creatures – Northern Scotland'.

For Young Writers' latest mini saga competition, we asked our writers to dig deep into their imagination and write a 100-word story with a beginning, middle and end, about a unique and original crazy creature; and the crazier the better!

The result is this collection of fantastic fiction with wild and whacky creations! Prepare for an adventure as you discover different dimensions with amazing alien life, mad mashed-up monster battles, cool superhero creatures, and why not befriend a fuzzy loveable beast? From the weird to the wonderful, there is something to suit everyone here.

There was a great response to this competition which is always nice to see, and the standard of entries was excellent, therefore I'd like to thank everyone who entered.

I hope you enjoy reading these stories as much as I did.

Keep writing,

Sarah Washer

CONTENTS

Freya Alexander (10)	57
Caitlin Anna Cox (10)	58
Joshua Reid (9)	59
Ava Clark (10)	60
Matthew George Young (11)	61
Shayan Safari (8)	62
Lauren May Winterburn (10)	63
Natalia Sabina Panka (10)	64
Ellis Clark (9)	65
Matt Dennis (11)	66
Holly Henderson (10)	67
Jessica Somers (9)	68
Finlay Haworth (11)	69
Kayla Ewens (10)	70
Owen Swanson (10)	71
Carly Michelle Dunlop (10)	72
Megan Kerr (11)	73
Cameron Robert Christie (10)	74
Mairi Gordon (10)	75
Kallie Davidson (9)	76
Georgia Mather (10)	77
Caitlin Poppy Shanaghey (9)	78
Callum Bruce (10)	79
Ava Buckley (8)	80
Isla Starkey (10)	81
Megan Lyndsey McCue (10)	82
Holly Thomson (11)	83
Amber Leith (9)	84
Jake Herd (11)	85
Zoe McDougall (8)	86
Holly Page (10)	87
Lyla Craggs (9)	88
Adam Duthie (11)	89
Adam Cowie (9)	90
Caitlyn Leonard (9)	91
Ross Stark (10)	92
Jack Reid (11)	93
Joel Ingram (10)	94
Hollie Marr (9)	95
Joshua Matthews (10)	96
Daniel Brodie Craigmile (9)	97
Cara Harvey (10)	98
Louise Sophie Brewis (10)	99

Raphael Mekhail (10)	100
Carrie Faith Emslie (10)	101
Alix Robertson (8)	102
Ella Mitchell (9)	103
Neve MacDonald (10)	104
Ruairidh Smith (11)	105
Mason Philip Davies (9)	106
Sophie Tait (11)	107
Kyle Stevenson (9)	108
Kayla Maya Brodziak (9)	109
Emma Stuart (9)	110
Calum Thomson (10)	111
Nathan Mbaeru (10)	112
Lauren Hay (10)	113
Louie James Goldie (10)	114
Alisha Louise Allan (10)	115
Finlay Bain (9)	116
Freya McCabe (10)	117
Kieran Hunter (10)	118
Kendel Laing (10)	119
Cara Brown (9)	120
Dylan James Young (9)	121
Ellis Glennie (9)	122

Glendelvine Primary School, Perth

Marnie Grace Williams (10)	123
Rosalie Thirsk (9)	124
Joel Hepburn (9)	125
Eve Errington-Goulty (8)	126
Megan Berry (8)	127
Eilidh Williamson (10)	128
Innes Murdo Liddle (9)	129

Portessie Primary School, Buckie

Cerys Goodall (11)	130
Joe Murray (10)	131
Catie Carter (11)	132
Jasmine Castel (9)	133
Isla Coull (11)	134
Eden Wojcik (10)	135
Courtney Grant (10)	136
Regan Duncan (11)	137

Marcus Wilson (11)	138
Archie Chalmers (10)	139
Amy Imlach (10)	140
Jude Addison (11)	141
Freya Grant (10)	142
Logan Wood (10)	143

Eli Thomas Barron (10)	174
Abbie Todd (9)	175
Layan AlHamdan (8)	176
Liam Neave (8)	177

Portlethen Primary School, Aberdeen

Leo Tonsic (11)	144
Fraser Haydn Cardno (10)	145
Julia Bugdal (10)	146
Luke Robert Scotson (10)	147
Arran Coull (10)	148
Ethan John Saum (10)	149
Mia Louise Donald (10)	150
Grant Lindsay (10)	151
Holly McPherson (10)	152
Kornelia Bartnicka (10)	153
Taylor Jane Stephen (10)	154
Olivia Jackson (10)	155
Liam Macarthur (10)	156
Kai Watson (10)	157
Megan Mary Farley (10)	158
Kieran Strachan (10)	159
Heather Lloyd (10)	160

Viewlands Primary School, Perth

Marnie Nye (8)	161
Murray William Leckie (9)	162
Campbell Shaw (10)	163
Sam McTeague (8)	164
Francesca Mudd (9)	165
Lewis Dyson (9)	166
Ava Stewart (9)	167
Emma Pryor (9)	168
Ocean-Melodie McCole (8)	169
Amelia Hutchison (9)	170
Modou Bah (8)	171
Alistair John MacGregor Milne (9)	172
Annabel Humphrey (9)	173

THE STORIES

Chaos In The Bedroom

Katy was just coming home to watch Amazing Archie Apple. She was just going to switch on the TV when...

For a moment she wished she had bravery, because she heard an eerie noise upstairs, but she went upstairs anyway. She grabbed her brother's Nerf gun. 'Who's there?' she called.

'No one,' came back a rough voice.

'I will come in.'

'You will be scared.'

Katy ran in.

'Do you want munchings and crunchings?'

Katy screamed like wind.

'I'm Gurg.'

'I-I'm Katy,' stammered Katy. Gurg was scared. 'Go away!' shouted Katy.

'No!' argued back Gurg!

'I will call the cops.'

Greg MacDougall (9)
Arisaig Primary School, Arisaig

Sports Day In The Deep Blue Sea

The Octo Squad were swimming super fast. It was sports day in the deep blue sea. Everyone was competing against the Dolphin Squad because no one liked them. 'OK children, time for the swimming race. Please line up against the wall.'
'OK Dolphin Squad, we're going to kick your butt.'
'We'll see about that.'
'3, 2, 1, swim!'
'Octo Squad has won the race. Congratulations Octo Squad.' The Octo Squad swam onto the podiums and got their medals and trophies. Dolphin Squad was so mad at their performance for not winning the race. 'Told you we would win the race!'

Breágha Millar (11)
Arisaig Primary School, Arisaig

Attached

Fairy Forgetmenot was the most appealing, bewitching fairy in the planet. She changed into a flower and the aroma was beyond compare, it was excellent. Her love, Ren, was impeccable. She loved him so much. 'Tootsie, help, I'm attached to him but I don't know if he loves me in the same way,' she explained. She was deeply in love. Ren was picking flowers as elegant as ballet dancers to give to Rose.

Ren knocked on Rose's door. 'What!' Rose bellowed.

'I brought you flowers as sweet as you,' Ren replied.

'Give them to someone who cares, like Forgetmenot.'

Corran Fiona MacKenzie (10)
Arisaig Primary School, Arisaig

Big Ben Bang!

Slimy was an ugly, but kind monster. His friend Gurgi was like an octopus vampire. Pencilman could draw out anything.

One day Slimy and his friends went to Earth to get away from Red (the evil monster).

Back on Earth, little Emily was playing on a bright, colourful swing. Then... Spaceship! Slimy and his friends crashed into Big Ben. They stepped out and saw Red about to blow up Big Ben. *Boom!* Nooo!' said Gurgi. Pencilman had a great idea: draw Big Ben back to life! Red decided to say sorry. Now Red, Slimy, Pencilman and Gurgi were best friends.

Chloe Jacqueline Harkins (9)

Arisaig Primary School, Arisaig

Adventure With Nelly

Nelly was a naughty monster and her favourite thing to do was adventure round the park. She liked swinging on the vines (the swings). She loved walking across the bridge of ice (the wobbly bridge). And Nelly was particularly good at climbing up the dangerous mountains (the climbing frame). Nelly also liked adventuring at the beach. She liked dragging herself across the boiling, hot desert (the sand). She enjoyed splashing around in the rapid rivers (the sea). She even trekked across the spiky rocks of doom (the rock pool). At the end of the day she went back to camp...

Hannah Muthel Gibb (11)
Arisaig Primary School, Arisaig

A Message To You All

Zane was a humble creature that was smaller than a pea, but braver than a flea. One day Zane met a clever camel. The camel said, 'How do you do?' Zane couldn't talk so he just nodded; he didn't know how. So the camel gifted him the power to speak. Zane still felt sad, so he went to the wisdom waterfall which gave him the power of strength and Zane said, 'Thanks, wisdom waterfall.' Zane then realised he didn't need these powers to find a friend. All creatures liked him the way he was. Your weaknesses are your strengths.

Teigan White (11)
Arisaig Primary School, Arisaig

Planet Home

It was a stormy day on Mars, the aliens could just see Earth on the horizon. On Mars there lived an alien called Marsh. He lived in a small crater with his sister Sara.

The next day came, Marsh just got home from fixing sewers! Sara persuaded Marsh to go to Earth! They hopped in the saucer pro, fastened their clipnogecs and left.

Seven months later they had seen wonderful things like: humans, flowers, water and more, but they had to go. On the way home they saw a planet. They called it Samarsh, they lived there instead. It's home.

Poppy Dennis Orchard (10)
Arisaig Primary School, Arisaig

Shadow

When I was a little girl I didn't need to hide in the shadows. But now I do need to hide in the shadows, because a giant came and nearly ate me. The giant had a big mouth and it looked like a dragon. Luckily, I was near some trees so I flew over to them. The giant followed me into the trees. When the creature was gone I came out. There was nothing in sight, not even a sound. I didn't know where the giant was, and I felt relieved. Finally, I could fly free to go away, home.

Maisie Cameron (8)
Arisaig Primary School, Arisaig

Scark Vs Igor - The Final Battle

'Ah!' sighed Scark. He was on his way home after being on holiday on the planet Holidays for two days. *I can't wait till I get home*, thought Scark. Suddenly Scark's pod crashed into something hard. *Woah*, thought Scark. When Scark stepped out of the pod, he saw rock, very hard, dark, black rock. *Igor's taken over*, thought Scark. Soon he found Igor's castle. *This is it*, thought Scark. Soon Scark's and Igor's armies were at war. In a matter of minutes Igor was defeated. 'Earth is back,' said Scark. Scark was finally home. 'Home at last,' said Scark, relieved.

Aiden Beattie (10)
Burrelton Primary School, Blairgowrie

Zoo-Zaka And The Villain Of Meanness

Zoo-Zaka was in his cave eating his yummy jellyblobs when all of a sudden, *scream!* Zoo-Zaka looked out of his cave and saw his cousin hanging by ropes! A villain tied her up! Zoo-Zaka ran and electrified this mysterious villain! Zoo-Zaka jumped to rescue her! However, this villain captured him! Zoo-Zaka was weak! 'Help!' he cried, but no one could save him. Zoo-Zaka remembered his strength power! He released himself and and his cousin! They ran! The villain's too weak to run! They both go back to Zoo-Zaka's cave and finish jelly. 'Thanks Zoo-Zaka.' They lived happily ever after!

Ailsa Mitchell (10)
Burrelton Primary School, Blairgowrie

The Adventure Of George And John To Justice

There was once a little onion bunion called Georgina-Morlena, George for short. One glorious little day on the planet Clubo, George was happily walking down the road, when he came across a storm-breaker, unfortunately he was only a puppy and shattered his own wing. Weirdly all of his family were leaving him alone homeless, cold and scared...

A little later George went up to the little white-winged, wiggling storm-breaker, wrapped him in a fluffy sheep blanket and took him home. George's home was magnificent, he had very colourful rooms. George called the storm-breaker John and they lived together in peace.

Ruby Stevenson (11)
Burrelton Primary School, Blairgowrie

The Wrestling Bug

Suddenly there is a loud crash. Gosty falls from the sky. He sees a sign, on it is 'Wrestling tomorrow at 9.15.' Gosty says that he wants to play, but he is a monster, so it will be pretty hard.

The next day, 'Woo hoo!' said Gosty, 'it is the day that I can wrestle.' Gosty asks to play tonight's game. 'Of course you can. You will be up against Gloopy.'

'Goody,' said Gosty, 'this will be fun.'

Up next Gloopy and Gosty...They wrestled for two hours. Then, 'We have a winner and the winner is... Gosty!'

Amy Martin (9)
Burrelton Primary School, Blairgowrie

Igor's Surprise

One day a griffin soared through the Highlands of Scotland, in and out the hills in search of food. His name was Igor, he squawked with delight.

Igor turned around and eyed up a small rabbit and he dived. The rabbit was in sight. Igor's claws were raised, he was just about to grab it when Migert (Igor's neighbour and bully) swooped in and took the rabbit. 'Hey, that's mine,' said Igor looking at Migert.

'Well you snooze you lose,' said Migert flying away.

The next day Igor went to look for Migert, he found him in a bog...

Brodie Fitzpatrick (10)
Burrelton Primary School, Blairgowrie

Chickens

'Ha, ha, caught you chicken number three.' Out in the country was a superhero who faked his own death because he was weak. So he started to do chicken catching.

30 years later, *trrrr.* 'Wow, it's an earthquake. I am Billy Bob, I am going to save the world again, yeah! I better get up. Cape, check. Face mask, check. Epic shoes, check. Let's go fight.' Mr Billy Bob went to help the people of the earthquake. He flew to central New York to help. It had lots of people who would probably not survive, which is sad.

Jamie Orr (10)
Burrelton Primary School, Blairgowrie

Slug's Bad Day

Slug the YouTuber was sitting on his leaf as happy as could be, filming his latest video about leaves, when the evil mastermind, Crow, came and picked Slug up. Quickly, he took him to his evil lair, locked him in a cage and lit the fire. 'Roasted slug for my tea, yum, yum.'
Then with his super powered campervan driving, Slug jumped out of the window into the campervan. Then hitting 100mph, he drove away to his leaf to finish his video. But then suddenly he saw Barbie and Ken having a picnic on his leaf. *Noooo!*

Sophie Hamilton (10)
Burrelton Primary School, Blairgowrie

The Unlikely Mission

One night, a meteor hit Earth and a strange creature came out. His name: Cat. His mission: get all the ancient relics. But he had to learn how to spell them first, but he hated teachers, so he decided to learn from another student. What could go wrong? Cat found a student and asked him how to spell Tutankhamun's tomb, but instantly the student turned to stone and ripped apart. Cat thought he'd become a teacher, that's why he turned to stone and ripped apart. Cat thought he had to get home, but he needed time fuel...

Michael Leonard Morris (10)
Burrelton Primary School, Blairgowrie

Vlad

Vlad was minding his own business when he was swooped up by William. The big bully William took Vlad to his nest. Vlad was being grabbed by his horns and finally Vlad was dropped. He shivered in fear, he was hungry, even more hungry by the minute. William came back ready to hurt Vlad, but Vlad shape-shifted into an egg, William flew away and Vlad transformed into himself again. Even hungrier than ever. He had an idea. He rushed around and built a model of himself. William came back and tried to land but the nest was gone.

Jessica Johnston (10)
Burrelton Primary School, Blairgowrie

Gloopy Meets His Worst Nightmare!

One day, in the middle of Scare Street, there lived a gloopy monster and one day Gloopy saw Gosty. Gosty had blue wings and pink bony rainbow arms and he was wrestling him tomorrow morning, at the wrestling match in Perth. In the middle of the night Gloopy got scared. He didn't really want to fight Gosty. Gosty was really nice, so he decided he was not going to fight him! That morning Gloopy went to the match, but no one was there. He looked all over the studio and then he looked up!

Lilli Buchan (9)
Burrelton Primary School, Blairgowrie

Mr Evil Worm's Horrendous Evening

Mr Evil Worm was taking a stroll underground. The rain was battering down. There was a sudden thump from the top. A paw came through the ground and grabbed Worm! Worm was taken away to an evil lair and was shown to another baddy. 'Ha! We finally got him!' shrieked Mickey Mouse and Pudsy. They tied Worm to a rope and Mickey ate him! Worm travelled round Mickey and then found a hatch! He opened it and jumped out. Unfortunately it was the back end of Mickey. Worm then did the force on both of them and then ran out.

Ellie McMartin (10)
Burrelton Primary School, Blairgowrie

Miracletoad Down The Plug

One day Miracletoad was wandering around his house and then he went for a swim in the sink and got sucked down the plug in the sewers, he was very scared. Then he heard something. He screamed, it was just Sewertoad. 'Hi Sewertoad.'
'Hi. I see you're stuck in the sewers.'
'Yes I am Sewertoad. I need help.'
'Well I can help you. Here's a teleporter.'
'Thanks, and bye. Wow! I am back home, hi Mum and Dad, I am home and I am also very hungry.'

Scott Jack (9)
Burrelton Primary School, Blairgowrie

A Big Problem

It was a nice day on Snot Planet, when suddenly there was a big crash that flooded the planet in the distance. Snot Girl zoomed to the planet, it was called Pencil Planet. It has pencils everywhere. She saw the foggy stuff clearing over the planet. She zoomed over to it and tried to push it away, but it was too sticky. She zoomed to the other planet called Rubby. She grabbed a rubber and took it away and rubbed out the sticky stuff, it worked, she was so pleased that she saved the day, so she went home.

Annie Watson (8)
Burrelton Primary School, Blairgowrie

Untitled

Bang! As I crashed into the desert. 'Aah, what is that big, moving thing?' I jumped on top of it. I went for an hour until I came to a forest. I jumped down into the forest and saw two people. I went over and I said, 'Do you want to be friends.' They said sure. I told them about Glopy and Beapy, they would help me to defeat Glopy and Beapy. At that moment we all saw Glopy and Beapy. We ran as fast as we could and we defeated Glopy and Beapy. 'Yeah!' we all shouted.

Jack Smith (9)
Burrelton Primary School, Blairgowrie

Pancake Escape!

So our story starts with this thing, Pancake Man, he is a pancake with arms and legs.

One day he got taken into a big van, nothing was stopping him getting out! *Bang*, he was out in a flash, he was amazingly strong. So he roamed around the city, he was very thirsty so he just drank syrup out of his syrup gun. But then he stopped, he saw this place called Pancake Camp, so he went into Pancake Camp and had fun. Suddenly, he thought to himself, *will I find the factory again?*

Logan Patton (8)
Burrelton Primary School, Blairgowrie

Millie And Moo

One cold night, a thing dropped from the sky and fell to the freezing cold sea of Slipsland. That thing was me. I'm Millie, I'm a mermaid. I'm normally in Mythical Mermaid Moon, but the smallest has to go and learn more about the world. Now I'm sitting on a rock in the middle of the sea. As I was playing ball I felt as if something was watching me. I turned to see a super, scary sea lion was watching me. I did not know what to do so I asked it to be my friend and it said yes.

Isla Ferriday (9)

Burrelton Primary School, Blairgowrie

Music Monstre's Quest

One day Music Monstre was playing his music when Music Hater came and threw his instruments all around the Planet of Sound. Monstre knew he had to go on a quest to get them back. First he went to the top of Mount Sard and found his drums. Then he went to the ocean and found his saxophone. Then he went into a deep, dark cave and found his cymbals. He went to Music Hater's cave and defeated him in a big battle and he was never bullied by him again, he actually became friends with him.

Marcus Preece (9)
Burrelton Primary School, Blairgowrie

Porky, The Pig Who Farts Glitter

It was just a normal day on the farm and Porky the pig was running away from the farmer who was trying to kill him, but Porky made a big mistake. He ran next door (into the toxic waste management centre) and stupidly hid in toxic goo. He turned into a one-hundred-eyed pig with wings, and he shot rainbows out of his butt. He even farted glitter. But Chief Blobby Bobby tried to capture him for an eye! Would Porky survive? To be continued...

Emma-Louise Wilkie (10)

Burrelton Primary School, Blairgowrie

Fire Cat!

Hi, I am Firecat. I live on Fire Island by myself. I have not yet explored the island. I think I hear someone talking. I don't know what to say, it didn't like me, it tried to spray me with fire. It looked the same as me. I used my powers by spraying it with fire, so if it chased me, its feet would burn. Suddenly a big crash happened because we shot fire at each other and then we looked at each other and we both were water creatures.

Finlay Wilson (9)
Burrelton Primary School, Blairgowrie

The Long Walk

One day, Mr Cat Man goes for a long walk and he goes so far that he walks straight into an eagle. So he asks the eagle where he is. The eagle tells him he's in Bird Land and only birds live there. So he walks on a little further through the mud and he meets a wizard. The wizard tells Mr Cat Man that to get home, he must find a key. He goes to a key he sees in the rock and opens the door and celebrates with his friend and has fun back at home.

Luke Sellen (10)
Burrelton Primary School, Blairgowrie

The Mission To Go Back Home

One day, Four Eyes was driving the spaceship and it crashed into Earth. He went outside and his enemies were coming up to him. He ran and ran until his legs couldn't run anymore. He went to his spaceship and went inside.
In the morning Four Eyes set to work to mend his spaceship. He was hungry, so he went to the forest and Four Eyes never found any food. So he went to the spaceship and he fixed it and Four Eyes zoomed off into space.

Rebecca Hamilton (8)
Burrelton Primary School, Blairgowrie

Anger Time

My name is Circle Whirly Girl, I am going to fight my brother, I am going to fight him because he took my phone. I fought him till he got hurt, he went crying. It took place in my house and the time was 9.15. I went in to my ball and my brother threw my phone at me and I was unhappy, so we went outside and fought again. I didn't win so I said, 'Let's have another fight.' So we did, it went on forever. In the end I won but I said sorry.

Holli Kirstie Grant (10)
Burrelton Primary School, Blairgowrie

Dilly Dally

Suddenly, *crash*, I fall to the ground and I find myself in a large city standing on the road. Suddenly a car comes racing up and stops right in front of me, he gets out of his car and puts me on the pavement. Soon I find a shop called 'Dilly Dally', then I open the door and a lady appears at the door and I find out she is a monster that can teleport. She took a hold of me and teleported me to the moon, then she went back.

Georgia Fraser (8)

Burrelton Primary School, Blairgowrie

I Am Hungry

One day there was a creature called Super Fast Crazy Jo. He went out for a walk to get something to eat. He saw something to eat and he started to run so fast and bumped into a tree. He got knocked out and somebody took him to a lake. When he woke up nobody was there. He went for a look around. Then he saw his house and ran to it super fast and bumped into a tree. He was so dizzy, he went into his house and bumped into his sofa.

Fraser Stuart Stark (8)
Burrelton Primary School, Blairgowrie

School Days

'Wake up Buffalo, you have got school.'
'Why?'
'Because you need to learn.'
'Why can't I skip school?'
'Because you have skipped school for five weeks.'
'Oh fine, but you have to get me a chocolate
pudding at the shop.'
'It's a deal.'
'Okay, get dressed.'
Ding, dong. 'Oh, hi Jake. You'd better go.'

Mollie Clark (9)
Burrelton Primary School, Blairgowrie

The Golden Model

When Music Eye was playing the guitar, he was hungry, so he went to the famous music world forest to get food, when he found something glowing, he went close to the glowing thing. It was a chest, he looked inside, he found gold and he took this gold and gave it to his mom to keep it safe for a week.

After a week he gave it to a wizard to make something out of it, like a model. He said, 'Get me more,' and he did it.

Leigh-Anna Robertson (9)

Burrelton Primary School, Blairgowrie

Action Man

One day there were two men that hated each other, then Slippy Bob shot waffles at the two men that hated each other. Slippy Bob made the men talk. They never listened to him.

The next day they didn't go near each other. The day after they didn't hate each other, they became friends forever.

Dylan Ferrier (9)
Burrelton Primary School, Blairgowrie

Untitled

Diggy was in the forest. This alien came along. He got really scared of the alien. The alien jumped out of the tree and gave him a fright. He asked, 'Would you like to be my friend?'
And Diggy said, 'Yes.'
The alien said, 'Can I come in your house to visit you?' They became best friends. The alien asked, 'Could I play in your bedroom with you and have a sleepover?'
Diggy said, 'Yes.'

Shauna Stewart (8)
Craighill Primary School, Tain

The Day That The Monster Turned Nice

One day a monster from London came to town. He looked fierce. He attacked a girl. He was pulling her, she fell off. He tried to eat her. She was sore. Zoomba was his name. Zoomba was very happy, but he hated humans. Zoomba drank a cup of water, he turned nice. He shook her hand, he let go and ran outside and jumped on the trampoline. He ran back inside. He wanted to turn mean again, so he drank some more, but he stayed the same and he cried, he was upset.

Zoe McDermid (7)
Craighill Primary School, Tain

Friendship

Once there was a monster called Kyi and he was made of fire. He could throw fireballs further than a catapult and he was in the forest when he heard a crunching sound on a stick. He was not alone! There was another monster called Slimer. He was made of slime and he could spit slime at other monsters. They made friends right away and soon they built a house out of bricks and cement in the forest. They lived there together for ever and ever.

Alexander W Gallie (7)
Craighill Primary School, Tain

The Best Day Ever

There was a giant mastermind, he was called the Devourer of Earth. He was eleven years old and he was so cool. He had a friend called Max. He was pretty cool. He could do a front flip and a back flip. The Devourer felt so happy that he cheered loudly, so that everyone heard. 'That was amazing!' he said.
Max said, 'I know!'

Jamie Greenlees (8)
Craighill Primary School, Tain

The Best Fight Ever

Once there was a monster, his name was Jaz and he had no one to fight and he was heading for a city. In the city there was another monster, his name was Gregor. Jaz turned bad and Gregor turned bad too. They were fighting Bob and Jaz and Gregor won and so they had no one to fight. They fought humans and the army came to fight. They brought tanks!

Nathan Wallace (7)
Craighill Primary School, Tain

Frog Monster

One day a little boy was in the woods. He saw a hat. It was on the ground. He put it on. He turned into a monster, it was a frog. He saw an evil Cyclops. He was chasing the boy. Frog Monster got smacked. Frog Monster was knocked out. A spotty snake saw Frog, the snake made him come back alive. 'Yeees!' He thanked him.

Reece Campbell (7)
Craighill Primary School, Tain

The Teacher's Surprise

One night, space exploded and Fred's mum and dad sent him to Earth. He landed in a school.
In the morning he hid in a corner when the teacher went for tea. He sat on the teacher's chair. And then he messed up the teacher's desk. Then he tied the teacher to the wall and he began to teach the class.

Jasmine Ronni Nicholson (7)
Craighill Primary School, Tain

Red's Dream

There lived a monster, he lived in a forest.
Everyone was scared of Red. Red was sad. One day
he saw another monster, it was a girl monster. She
was beautiful. Red walked up to her, they were
friends.
Two weeks later they were married.

Grace Bruce (7)
Craighill Primary School, Tain

The Champion Robot

There was a scrap yard. That night the new robot boxer came. It was the new champion. No one could defeat him. Then the best came. He got defeated. Then the other robot was really sad. He went back to the forest and cried.

Mackenzie Ross (7)

Craighill Primary School, Tain

Monster At The Shop

One day Shellman was counting the shelves; what a lot of shelves! He wondered how many there were. He was as quiet as a mouse because he was scared. He had not been in a shop before. He had to go home because it was late.

Aaron Fraser Mackenzie (6)
Craighill Primary School, Tain

The Sad Monster

One day a monster came to town. The monster scared the people. They ran home. The monster was all alone, the monster was sad. She wanted a friend. She left, the monster never came back.

Grace Twemlow (7)
Craighill Primary School, Tain

Untitled

It was a scary night, Fluffy Monster played around. She went home, her mum let her play on the iPhone. She played Frozen and she went to bed because she was tired.

Katie-Lana Jade Clydesdale (8)

Craighill Primary School, Tain

Blonglong The Amazing

One day Blonglong got a call. 'Help! Our teacher is trying to make us do homework and there's only one week left.'
Blonglong sat up and ran out of the door. 'I am coming!'
A few minutes later Blonglong arrived, he sneaked into the classroom and watched for a while, then when all the pupils went out of class he jumped out and scared the teacher. 'You shall not give the poor pupils homework!'
'Yes Master.' Blonglong hypnotised the teacher. When the pupils found out, they knew only one monster could do this, his name was Blonglong. Amazing!

Hannah Lyons (11)
Deanston Primary School, Deanston

Bad Bee: Three Steps Of Annoying

Have you seen the bad bee? The bad bee goes round everywhere, from noisy cities to quiet villages. He goes round only doing three things, number one: buzzes round and round annoying the person to death. Number two: goes to eyes right in front of them, just making them more and more angry, because you know you would get fed up if a fly was around your eyes! Finally, what you've all been waiting for, number three: it stings, probably the worst thing a bee can do to you, especially if crazy people let loads of bees sting them.

Paul Smith (11)
Deanston Primary School, Deanston

Horn And The Bullies

One day, Horn was walking home from school, through the woods, when he heard a stick break behind him. He was frightened, so he started running but then Horn heard whispers coming from the trees, he stopped running and listened in the direction it was coming from. He saw three bullies from his school, that's when he realised they were trying to scare him. Horn shouted, 'Go away, I'm not scared.' Horn didn't care, he ignored the bullies and walked the rest of the way home, feeling brave.

Rebecca Stewart (8)
Deanston Primary School, Deanston

Return Of Petripeng

Kingpeng and all the penguins were having a good day enjoying the nice Antarctic ice but then Kingpeng saw Petripeng, who had returned from the dead. Petripeng was an evil polar bear-eating, monster penguin who was as fast on land as he was in water, and he wanted to be the leader of all penguins. He challenged Kingpeng to a battle in the ice arena. It was a tough battle, but in the end Kingpeng won and they made a deal that Petripeng had to stay away and never return. All penguins lived on.

Matthew Armstrong (10)

Deanston Primary School, Deanston

The Curse Of Monster Town

One night in Monster Town there was a monster called Andy and that night it was the third of March, which meant it was the curse night and that's when the bad monsters come out and scared the good monsters. So he was scared and worried because he had a great enemy, Barry, the three-eyed beast. So he barricaded his door and his windows and sat. Usually it started at 12.00, midnight and then he heard a bang. He thought he would be safe at home. Just then he heard a roar! He jumped out of his skin.

Scott Stewart (10)
Deanston Primary School, Deanston

Nothing Lasts Forever

'It's time to leave,' Waffle heard his best friend say. They were going away from everything where they grew up and their parents and siblings. 'Come on, we're leaving.' As they were leaving they heard *bang!* Waffle turned around, their home had been blown up. *Bang!* No! Chomp got blown up. A hooded figure walked up. 'Take me, you'll be doing me a favour.'

'No,' he replied.

'Do it Pancake.'

'I want to make you suffer even more first, mwahahaha.'

'What could you do to make me suffer? I've lost everything.'

'I will make you watch Waffle's kind die out.'

Marianne Coney (10)
Elrick Primary School, Westhill

Cantseeme Bedwatcher

It's time for kids to sleep. Cantseeme creeps into Alfred's bedroom. His long, four hairy legs crawled up the drainpipe. He looked around with his four long eyeballs. He found a comfortable place next to a beanbag. He huddled up his hairy, green body. Alfred kept fidgeting. He couldn't get very comfy. Cantseeme thought he was asleep but he wasn't. Alfred woke up and looked around. He spotted Cantseeme watching him sleep. Cantseeme tried to run but Alfred got up and chased Cantseeme. Cantseeme's tongue dragged along the floor leaving slobber. *Squish!* Alfred stamped on Cantseeme. That was him gone!

Amy Slesser (11)
Elrick Primary School, Westhill

Every Dragon Has A Talent!

The next morning Maleficent saw red, hot, fire smoke. It was the red, hot pepper dragon. If she opened her eyes, her eyes would burn and she would die. So she would have to do her Highland dancing with her eyes closed and the red hot pepper dragon would leave, oops! I forgot to tell you that she is a world champion Highland dancer. *Roar!* 'I can't stand your dancing.' T
hat was the end. Maleficent heard loads of screaming. 'It's the red hot pepper dragon, he's killing people. Maleficent will have to do her dancing, it's working.'
'Nooo! Argh! Never!'

Sophie Iona Sinclair (10)
Elrick Primary School, Westhill

Fireball

'Grrr! Why is nobody at the schools or shops? Now I have nobody to scare. It's unfair! I know, I'll search the funfair!' Fireball changed into a fireball and charged to the fair. 'Aaahhh!' about five hundred people screamed.

'Yes! They're scared!' He changed back to himself again and ran at 70mph across the fair, through queues punching, kicking and shooting lasers! Every single person at the fair was running so fast, but not fast enough because Fireball was so much faster! Finally everyone was gone so Fireball started eating all the candy floss and hot dogs! Then he walked home.

Ella McPherson (11)
Elrick Primary School, Westhill

Zog And The Game Console

Last week, Lucy and I were playing a game on my console called Zig Zag. My character was a small, blue, fluffy creature called Zog.
After an hour the game went black and out came Zog! 'Ahh!' Lucy and I yelled.
Zog said, 'Don't be scared, you need to pass five levels then my family can come back.'
'Why?' I said.
'Because you lost a level, now they're behind a wall.'
'We'll do it.'
Zog left, we played the game for two hours, lost the first, second, third and fourth round then, 'Yes, I did it!' Zog got her family.

Freya Alexander (10)
Elrick Primary School, Westhill

The Fight Of Friendship

Big, flexible, pink, strong, crazy Flexer was working out at the gym, when it suddenly got very warm. Flexer looked behind him and saw his enemy called Toasty. Flexer walked up to him. Flexer said, 'Do you want to have a fight?'
Toasty said, 'Yes.' Then the fight started. Toasty burned Flexer's face but Flexer lifted his leg to Toasty's tummy. Toasty was so scared he ran away. Then Flexer was so happy he started running around Mell Town shouting, 'I'm a winner, I'm a winner!' He walked in doing handstands around town. When he met Toasty, they said sorry.

Caitlin Anna Cox (10)
Elrick Primary School, Westhill

The Big Adventure

Once upon a time lived a worm named Fizzy. He was once playing the Xbox with Meli his best friend. They were playing the Xbox and then they got shot by a cannon; they were lost. 'No!' said Meli. Fizzy had fangs. Worms were crawling around. Then suddenly a giant bird started attacking them. 'No, don't eat me please, I taste horrible,' said Fizzy.

'OK, I won't eat you,' said the giant bird. 'I will take you home too,' said the giant bird.

'Yay, I'm going home,' said Fizzy. Later he played with Meli again. They lived happily ever after.

Joshua Reid (9)
Elrick Primary School, Westhill

Why Can't I Be Normal?

It was Blubble's first day at human school and he was very excited. Blubbles was a small, friendly creature so it was a big deal for him. The scary bell rang and he quickly ran into school. He had a lovely teacher, Mrs White. First thing they had was reading. Blubble loved reading, it was his favourite, but he couldn't focus today 'cause he was different. The scary bell rang for playtime. Blubble stood and watched kids play. He asked himself, *Why am I different?*
'It's good to be different,' someone said. Blubble thought it was good to be different!

Ava Clark (10)
Elrick Primary School, Westhill

Squiggle McBlob's Adventure

One morning in Shapeshifter Town, Squiggle McBlob was rushing to get to the McBlob bus. This was where it took you to Neptune. There are very dangerous creatures out there. Like Cyblobs and Squiggle Flamey. It took Squiggle McBlob an hour to get to Neptune. Neptune is a big, blue planet. Once he landed, he found that Cyblobs were all over Neptune. He saw on a sign: 'Wanted, Squiggle McBlob'. 'Over there,' said one of the Cyblobs, 'get him.'

'No!' said Squiggle McBlob. He shape-shifted into the floor so the Cyblobs could not see him.

Matthew George Young (11)
Elrick Primary School, Westhill

The Battle

Once there were two teams, Chunky Squad and Fishbirdy. They used to be friends but sadly they had an argument and that is where the story begins.

At war! The leader of Fishbirdy despised war, but they had to fight for their dignity. Fishbirdy despised the bloodshed but Chunky found it extremely amusing. Fishbirdy wanted Chunky to sign a peace treaty. Chunky said OK, but then Chunky back-stabbed him, and bombarded Fishbirdy's town. Fishbirdy thought there was only one way to end this bloodshed. It was to surrender, even though they definitely won, but Fishbirdy hated war and bloodshed.

Shayan Safari (8)
Elrick Primary School, Westhill

The World Of The Deep

My mum and I went swimming yesterday, our favourite activity. I swam around, jumped in and showcased my amazing diving. When I jumped in the pool something wrapped around my feet, when I looked it was... a Decapus smiling at me! 'Name's Frederick,' he said. Urgently I looked around and discovered an underwater world of luminous colour with ferocious sharks, old turtles and grazing seahorses adding to the variety. I was scared, but intrigued to find out more. I swam out to take a breath, then jumped back in. *Splash!* The sound I heard before I woke from my dream.

Lauren May Winterburn (10)
Elrick Primary School, Westhill

A Lifetime Adventure

Ronnie was taking a peaceful stroll through Fire Wood to calm down from her friends. Suddenly she got zapped with a really light blue ray which teleported her to Pluto. Everyone who lived there got a shock, they thought she was scary and ugly. There was one little kid who went up to her. The little kid said, 'Hello.'

So Ronnie said, 'Hello.'

The little kid shouted, 'This creature is nice!' Slowly everyone came back. The president greeted Ronnie and made her a friend of their kind. Ronnie loved playing with everyone. She thought they were very nice and helpful.

Natalia Sabina Panka (10)

Elrick Primary School, Westhill

Basherbomb Saves The Day

What is that noise? Basherbomb got out of bed and saw something out the window. It was about 24 feet tall with a massive head and legs. Basherbomb had to do something. Basherbomb went up to it and chopped off its leg, but the monster hit him. Basherbomb went so dizzy. Basherbomb got back to normal and climbed the monster. Basherbomb saw who was controlling it. Thunderbolt! He broke the glass and killed Thunderbolt. Everyone in Crazy Creature Village was cheering and dancing around crazily. They were all chanting, 'Basherbomb, Basherbomb, Basherbomb.' When he came down he was smiling.

Ellis Clark (9)
Elrick Primary School, Westhill

Untitled

Rock 'n' Roller comes from the asteroid that wiped out the dinosaurs. One day Rock 'n' Roller was bathing in the dense soil on a scorching day. He didn't feel it, as he'd entered the atmosphere at thousands of degrees in his past! Anyway, while he was bathing, miners pulled up in a truck! He started rolling at 30mph as he had no feet. One of the miners spotted Rock 'n' Roller and alerted his colleagues. Together, they pulled out sharp, gleaming pickaxes. They took a hit at him; nothing happened... he's indestructible! And that's the story of Double R!

Matt Dennis (11)
Elrick Primary School, Westhill

Evil Teacher Muncher

One ordinary day at a school, all of P6C were doing Maths and Miss Crockett was showing everybody what to do. Then suddenly the door swung open. In came Miss Crockett's evil sister, Evil Teacher Muncher. Miss Crockett shouted, 'Why are you here?'

'I wanted to see you. Come here now.'

'No! Children run!' All the children tried to run but they couldn't. Miss Crockett had a drink of tea, then became two. Then so did Evil Teacher Muncher. She had a drink of tea and became two. One Miss Crockett grabbed the children then the other started to fight.

Holly Henderson (10)

Elrick Primary School, Westhill

Plogo's Dream

Plogo is a baby Fluff Boom from Zemore. She is so cute, she can't scare anyone, so one day she tried to scare her enemy, her brother Blogo. She went to his room and went, 'Baaa!'

'So not scary sis, aww!'

So the next day she woke up and found a clown mask. Blogo hated clowns, so she went to his room, got his foghorn, pressed the button and shouted, 'Baa!'

'Get out of my room!'

'Yay, I got you.'

'Oh my Fluff Boom, you got me,' and Plogo never scared him again and they lived happily ever after.

Jessica Somers (9)
Elrick Primary School, Westhill

Krunk And The Nooting Noot

Krunk was looking round his scrapyard for upgrade pieces, when... *Boom!* Krunk turned his TV head sharply. What he saw surprised even him! But not for long, as he quickly fired at the huge beast in front. The creature thrashed and turned to Krunk. The teeth were frighteningly sharp and scary. Krunk ran forward and jabbed the creature, the blood was white! The creature thrashed again and bit Krunk! It went in for another bite, Krunk sidestepped. He killed it and was about to celebrate! Whoo! Krunk celebrated by looking for parts and got really, really strong!

Finlay Haworth (11)

Elrick Primary School, Westhill

Stolen Heart

A cat, Kitty Purry, had a stolen heart. She had no love. A bad cat, she accidentally walked into a heart-warming store. Kitty Purry bought cookies and ate them. She'd just realised that they were from a heart-warming store; it was too late, she transformed into a very nice cat! She had lots of friends now! She changed her looks and thoughts in one cookie. Kitty Purry loved the people she'd hurt more than the people she didn't hurt. From now on she buys those cookies every month because she loves her life! Kitty Purry finally has a beautiful heart!

Kayla Ewens (10)
Elrick Primary School, Westhill

Beans And Gnomes

Laser Bean was king of all the beans. He wanted his army to stand up to the gnomes. The gnomes were blue, green, red and all sorts of different colours. The gnomes were very immature, they wanted all of the treasure that the beans had. One day Laser Bean decided to see the king of the gnomes. Laser Bean didn't have to walk, he teleported! *Flash!* Laser Bean was in the castle. He saw the king next to him. Laser Bean used his lasers against the gnomes, the gnomes were scared and ran away. 'Hooray!' said the beans, 'We're safe.'

Owen Swanson (10)
Elrick Primary School, Westhill

The Disaster In Cotton Candy Land

Once upon a time there was a little creature named Fluffy Kluffy. She was very fluffy, she smelt like cotton candy. She had a pink bow and the rest of her was yellow.

Fluffy woke up to a loud bang outside. She looked out her window and realised she was in the human world! She walked outside. Humans were standing, staring at her. 'Hello there!' Fluffy said happily.

A few hours later they became really good friends. The humans helped Fluffy get back to Cotton Candy Land. Fluffy was very grateful. She thanked them, then went back to her home.

Carly Michelle Dunlop (10)
Elrick Primary School, Westhill

Cinnobun's First Day At School

One dull day in Cinnotown, Cinnobun was going to school and it was his first ever day at Cinnoman Primary School. When he got there, he hung up his coat and went into class, he was in P3C and he loved his teacher.

But one day he went outside for a snack and three other boys called Cinnomansugar, Cinnomansticks and Cinnomanpowder came up to him and called him names like 'Stinkybun'. Then at the end of the day Cinnobun told his parents and they said to ignore it.

The next day the bullies said, 'Sorry,' and then they became best friends.

Megan Kerr (11)
Elrick Primary School, Westhill

Enslaved

Nohair has no hair - people try to get him to grow hair but he doesn't want to, so one day when somebody tried to get him to grow hair, he used his three mouths to his advantage and ate him whole! *Chomp, chomp, chomp.*
Wowsers, that was fun, thought Nohair! 'Ouch,' the next hit was a hard one, it left another scar, so he enslaved him for all eternity and nowadays he has many scars. He can shape-shift into things which means he is practically unstoppable! *Gobbleyup, gobbleyup, gobbleyup*, he gobbles up lots of things!

Cameron Robert Christie (10)
Elrick Primary School, Westhill

Lab Accident

In a lab, at the centre of the Earth, the clever scientists of the world made a mistake with experiment X1034Z and the animals that they used merged together. This creature, part golden eagle, part hawk, part monkey and part panther, by the name of Chicius Maximillius (Chax for short), now roams the rainforests in search of prey. Prey like your children, your pets, your family! But of course he looks for other things too, because he loves fish (but who doesn't). From now on if you hear a scratching noise, put the fish on the doorstep OK!

Mairi Gordon (10)
Elrick Primary School, Westhill

Sabby's Days

Sabby woke up on a different planet, she
saw other monsters so she got up and went over
to them and then asked if she could be part of the
group, but they said no because she was too cute.
So the next day she went to them to say, 'Could I
join the group now?'
They still said, 'No, you're too cute.'
Then Sabby said, 'I will prove you wrong.' So then
she started shooting fireballs out her mouth, the
she stopped and said, 'Now can I be in the group?'
Then they said yes, then they played.

Kallie Davidson (9)
Elrick Primary School, Westhill

Chomp

Chomp had a friend called Waffle. One day Chomp and Waffle went for a walk and Waffle got eaten. Chomp kept walking and he bumped into Anti-Chomp. So when Chomp saw Anti-Chomp, Chomp made five trees fall down. After Chomp did that, Anti-Chomp fixed it. So Chomp bit Anti-Chomp and Anti-Chomp disappeared. Chomp is now a hero. Chomp got many medals for defeating other monsters. But one day Chomp ran into Shredder so Chomp bit Shredder in the chest. After that, Shredder disappeared. So then Chomp saw that Waffle was still alive. Chomp was so happy to see Waffle again.

Georgia Mather (10)
Elrick Primary School, Westhill

Roar The Un-Scary Monster

A long time ago instead of Westhill, there was Monsterville where five mean monsters stood, and that's where our story begins. Roar was a monster that always wanted to be part of the scaring team. He couldn't though, because he wasn't scary enough.

One day he was just walking, then he had an idea, he could plan the biggest scare in Monsterville history. He stayed up all night but he finished. When he had set up he got ready, he sneaked up behind them then roared. The monsters nearly jumped out their skin, so they agreed he could join in.

Caitlin Poppy Shanaghey (9)
Elrick Primary School, Westhill

The Multi Dragon

There was a Multi Dragon. It was multicoloured and had a lot of different features like seven eyes, fire breathing and more. It was a breathtaking dragon.

One day he wasn't very happy, so he decided to fly to Pluto and annoy them. Little did he know there was a giant, blue Minotaur called Protector who protected Pluto. Protector was far bigger than him. He kept on flying to Pluto but then Protector saw him and started to shout. Multi Dragon saw him, it was too late to do anything. Protector picked him up and threw him. Pluto was safe.

Callum Bruce (10)
Elrick Primary School, Westhill

Invisible Max

Once there was a creature called Max. He had ten eyes, four arms. He could turn invisible too. Max wasn't like the rest, one morning he decided to play with his friends that could turn invisible too. Then lots of people turned up. Then all of his friends turned invisible, so then he was the only one standing. It's not his fault that he looked like that. Everyone kept saying, 'You're evil.' Time to prove a point. So he started doing kind things to people and started helping people, then everyone liked Max. Then he went invisible.

Ava Buckley (8)
Elrick Primary School, Westhill

Chocchip The Cruncher Monster

Meet Chocchip, the cruncher monster. She loves chocolate chips. She is gentle if you don't have chocolate chips, but if you do, you're toast! She was born in Laser Land but she lives on the lovely, fancy food island. Her enemy is out-of-date chocolate, but her main one is Watermelon Fangs.

One day she got a text saying her enemy was out of jail, so she got into action and tracked him down. Then she sneaked up on him and took out one of his fangs. Suddenly, *bang!* He's on the ground and in the toughest town jail.

Isla Starkey (10)
Elrick Primary School, Westhill

The Power Of Cake!

On Tasty Food Island, Cakey Blob was happily making cake in the cake cafe for breakfast. The bell at the door tingled. Cakey looked behind her, it was Cookie Monsta, her good friend. Cookie Monsta ran towards her and started to stomp on all the cakes! Cakey had seen this before, he had eaten a mouldy cookie! She threw a cake at Cookie Monsta. She missed. Cakey threw another cake. It missed again. Cakey had one good cake left. She threw it up, praying it would land in Cookie Monsta's mouth. It did! Cakey Blob used the power of cakes!

Megan Lyndsey McCue (10)
Elrick Primary School, Westhill

Flufflee In Danger

Flufflee strolled along the sidewalk of Girly Pearl Planet. Well, she thought she was, see she was so fluffy she couldn't see anything apart from herself. She was walking on the east side of the planet, straight into her worst enemy, Cave Lee, the dragon. The last time she saw Lee she hypnotised him and he fell off a cliff. She walked in and Flufflee could feel the boiling heat of Lee's fire and hear the sound of his cave suddenly closing. She tried to hide but ended up hiding in the middle of the floor. Suddenly, in came Lee!

Holly Thomson (11)
Elrick Primary School, Westhill

The Battle

In the land of ice there was a mountain starting to appear.

One hundred years later Peplow was born. As she grew older, her species became endangered by the Gremlins. They wanted to take over the mountain. Then one day Peplow was looking into the water when she heard a crack in the ice. She turned around and saw a Gremlin. Quickly she shot a laser beam at the Gremlin. She shape-shifted into a rock. The king Gremlin was dead. All the other Peplows appeared from rocks and grass.

Peplow was the new queen of Peplows and their habitat was saved!

Amber Leith (9)
Elrick Primary School, Westhill

Dr Icicle

One day Dr Icicle was walking in the Antarctic Circle base. Then the alarm went off, everyone started running to their stations. Dr Icicle just stood still. He had no station because he was their spy guy. Then a big, metal plate fell on top of him and slammed him to the ground. He tried to use his strength to lift up the metal plate, but it was just too heavy. Then he remembered his frostbite eyes. Maybe if he used them to freeze the plate, then punch it, it would shatter. *Freeze! Punch!* The plate shattered, 'I'm free!'

Jake Herd (11)
Elrick Primary School, Westhill

Mr Puff

Mr Puff lives in Scarlind, in Scarlind it's all gloomy and dark, nobody likes Puff especially Mr Gupp. So Puff went for a little walk in Scarlind, he kept on walking until he saw a girl, her name was Miss Leap. Different words popped up, she is beautiful, clever, gentle and a mermaid to him. Now Puff didn't want to leave, so he asked her, 'Do you want to come with me to a different country and teach me how to be nice?'

'Of course,' Miss Leap said.

'Yes!' Puff shouted. Puff had a good life after all.

Zoe McDougall (8)
Elrick Primary School, Westhill

Scary Ruby

Moody Ruby was looking for a home and on her journey she jumped out and scared some people and pushed some people. She eventually found a home and started living in it. Moody Ruby had a job, it was to push and scare people and she did that every day.

After she had done it for fifty days, Moody Ruby wanted a rest, so she laid down on her rusted, sticky, gooey hard bed and hibernated for six days. A random monster came into her hole and said, 'Can I work with you?'

She moaned and eventually said, 'Yes, friend.'

Holly Page (10)
Elrick Primary School, Westhill

Meli's New Friend

Once upon a time there was a slug called Meli. He was short and cute. He lived in Terryland, a land of smartness. He had an enemy called the Technoguard.

One day Meli and his new friend, Fizzy the worm, played in the garden when suddenly the Technoguard jumped out. 'Oh no,' said Meli and Fizzy. But then the Technoguard waved his stick and flew away. 'What was that about? asked Meli. 'He is coming back,' said Fizzy. The Technoguard came back and fought. Meli and Fizzy won and went back to play in the garden.

Lyla Craggs (9)
Elrick Primary School, Westhill

Watch Out For The Wall

Suddenly, the stickiest, most craziest creature ever appeared. His name is Sticky Mickey and trust me, make sure he doesn't get stuck to the wall.
One day Mickey was walking on a ragged path, when suddenly he got stuck to a cracked, mud-infested wall. After that day he hated any type of wall. When he finally got free from that chipped wall, he swore he would never walk into a wall again. At that moment he realised how much power he had. He realised unfortunately for him, his nose fell off. He had to get a pig nose. Happy days.

Adam Duthie (11)
Elrick Primary School, Westhill

Alien Monster

Once there was a monster called Mastiro. He came from a planet called Farg, he was sent to Earth to care for humans, so he could learn about them. When he crash-landed there was a massive explosion. He started walking to find a home. After he walked a mile he found a house and he didn't think anyone was in, he was wrong. He heard a voice, he started to run until he bumped into his enemy, Lord Zerg. He trapped Mastiro in a cage but he turned himself into a key and unlocked the cage. They battled, Zerg lost.

Adam Cowie (9)
Elrick Primary School, Westhill

Veddryia V Snakergly War

Veddryia looked up at the sun and he knew what day it was; it was the day he battled it out with his enemy, Snakergly. Since they were young they always fought for victory, but this time it was different, they were battling for the throne. They walked onto the battlefield, they knew what was going to happen! Snakergly took a wedge kick which meant he was in the lead by a lot! Veddryia remembered his own power and suddenly whipped his finger and suddenly turned Snakergly into ice! And he was put into a museum for everyone to see!

Caitlyn Leonard (9)
Elrick Primary School, Westhill

The Big Chase

There was a scary person called Shredder. He had two enemies called Buster and Kung Fu. Shredder lived in Aberdeen in an underground base. One day he saw his enemies walking next to his base. A few minutes later he heard a big *smash!* He sprinted downstairs to see if anything had been stolen and there had; his cape! He sprinted after them, but they were about 25 metres away. He eventually caught them. A few minutes later the police arrived and they got shoved in the police car and taken away. Shredder got his cape back.

Ross Stark (10)
Elrick Primary School, Westhill

The Monstrous Moon Worm

The monstrous moon worm was slithering through the ground. He was gobbling up tasty moon rock. The he heard a rumbling below him. He wondered what it was... The tunnel exploded behind him. It was the vicious moon mole! The moon mole hated the moon worm. The moon mole sped off. The mole was in hot pursuit, but luckily the moon worm was faster, thanks to the aerodynamic spikes on his back. Moon Worm had an idea, he slithered really fast round and round. The moon mole got really dizzy and fell over in a daze. Moon Worm had won.

Jack Reid (11)
Elrick Primary School, Westhill

The Demon Conscience

Once upon a time there was a boy called James Grimer who loved football but whenever he got angry his demon conscience took over, hacked the players and got sent off.

One day the team entered a tournament and James went along but didn't play any games. They got in the final. He came on for five minutes. People made him so angry, it was 1-1. One minute left, he felt like hacking people but didn't! With five seconds left he ran and jumped, turned and overhead kicked it in to the top corner. He had won it!

Joel Ingram (10)

Elrick Primary School, Westhill

Story Of Eveeie

Hi! My name is Eveeie. I will tell you the story about the battle of the dicksie and me and how the dicksie is my enemy. I was just chilling in my room having fun. *Knock, knock*, I went to the door and saw the dicksie. I opened the door and said hi. The dicksie said, 'Hello, can I come in please?' 'Um, OK Dicksie, shut the door, now let's battle!' I shot fire at the dicksie and the dicksie said, 'I will get you next time!' and left. I was relieved. I never wanted to see her again.

Hollie Marr (9)
Elrick Primary School, Westhill

Mr Smiles

Mr Smiles was walking his dog, when Mr Frowns kicked his dog.

Later Mr Frowns stole Mr Fat's pie and laughed in his face, then Mr Fat and Mr Frowns started to make a big fight between the two of them, then they smashed the pie.

Next, Mr Fat chased Mr Frowns away to the mountains and quickly ran back to the local village.

Later that day Mr Smiles was hiking on that very same mountain that Mr Frowns was on. Out-of-luck Mr Smiles found Mr Frowns and he pushed him off the cliff. That's the end of Mr Frowns.

Joshua Matthews (10)
Elrick Primary School, Westhill

Slimy Stuff

Gloomy is a monster that has 1987 slimy tentacles. He uses them to walk around on land. He is blue, red and orange and has electric going from eye to eye. He is lost and can't find his home because of his evil brother, Gloome! He is not alone because of his best friend. Gloome has two legs and 50 wings. He is black, red and slimy. They finally found their home but who was guarding it... Gloome! *Zap! Clang! Bang! Kapow!* He fell off the rooftop he was standing on, but he is still here. Dun! Dun!

Daniel Brodie Craigmile (9)
Elrick Primary School, Westhill

Purple Head

Purple Head was walking along the very long tunnel underground on the way out of her house, her pellets banging off the walls. She was on the way to meet her enemy. Purple Head had approached the end of the tunnel and hoisted herself up to the strange world she lived in and there was Mr Dragon. 'Are you ready to fight now?' he said.

'Yes I am.' The fight started straight away but it was not on for long, because Mr Dragon had to go because he was injured. So after, Purple Head ran home to tell her family.

Cara Harvey (10)
Elrick Primary School, Westhill

Sticky Steve's Magical Adventure

Sticky Steve was walking down Sticky Road with his multicoloured antennae bopping up and down, his big, bright, purple eye shining in the sunlight and his arms and legs in a twist. Whilst he was out walking he saw a door. He went through the door and magically he was in a jungle. He saw that his enemy, Invisible Isla had followed him. They hated each other and started fighting. Suddenly Sticky Steve saw the door he entered by. He went through it and Invisible Isla didn't see where he went and she was stuck in the jungle.

Louise Sophie Brewis (10)

Elrick Primary School, Westhill

Pancaker Vs Waffle

One day Pancaker left his only home, which is Maple Syrup Land, to go out into the world where he hoped to beat his enemy, the Waffle, in a 'who's the tastier' battle. When he arrived they asked people to lick them to see. Of course Pancaker won, but then a boy loved Waffle's taste so it was a tie between them. So they asked a man called Chomper to taste them but he ate both of them and neither could get out. So they decided to make friends in Chomper's stomach, even though no one won their taste battle.

Raphael Mekhail (10)
Elrick Primary School, Westhill

Creature Gets Caught

Punch is in Zoogel shopping, but all he can think about is his enemy Goggle, he is having so many dreams about him. But he just keeps on shopping. Then he saw a little glimpse of his enemy, so Punch decided to follow him to a secret location. Guess where it was? Under the mall. He caught Goggle's green hand and locked him up. He didn't know he would get him, but he left so he got the chance to get loose. It was easy for Goggle to get the lock. He got out, so Zoogel might see him again.

Carrie Faith Emslie (10)

Elrick Primary School, Westhill

Candy Princess

Once upon a time there was a girl called Princess Pinkie, she was the princess of Candy Land, her enemies were King Bat, Prince Cat and Prince Rat. They always bugged her, but her guards always saved her. Princess Pinkie went on a walk by herself. Suddenly she heard a loud bang, the lollipop streetlight went off. It was King Bat. Luckily she could fly, so she flew to the castle and locked herself in her castle and told her guards to kill them and they did, so she was safe. She lived happily ever after.

Alix Robertson (8)
Elrick Primary School, Westhill

The Battle Of Fart Man And Murder Man

Fart Man is walking along the road, when he sees Murder Man down the street murdering all types of crazy creatures all over town. Fart Man wonders if he will survive. Murder Man spied Fart Man, so he raced over to Fart Man. Murder Man knocked Fart Man over. Fart Man had fainted.

When Fart Man woke up, Murder Man had a knife in his hand. Fart Man immediately stood up and farted. Murder Man was on the floor, he had fainted. Fart Man told Police Boy to lock Murder Man up before he woke up. Fart Man saved everyone.

Ella Mitchell (9)

Elrick Primary School, Westhill

The Defeat Of Dark Eye

Spyro went out for a walk in the woods and suddenly he bumped into Dark Eye. Spyro decided to fight, but Dark Eye disappeared before Spyro could do anything, so he went home.

The next day Spyro travelled to Dark Town where Dark Eye lived and fought him until he died.

The next day he went to Dark Eye's house to collect all the belongings and saw a ghost. When he got closer he saw that it was Dark Eye's ghost so he burned him to the ground. Spyro went back to Spiral Town forever and ever.

Neve MacDonald (10)
Elrick Primary School, Westhill

Fangs And The UK

Fangs came to the UK on holiday. It was sunny, but not as sunny as the Sahara Desert where he came from. Fangs decided to stay! He started at the local school. On his first day he got... homework! He ran outside! But it was raining! Those two things were his worst nightmare. He ran back inside and saw the homework, so he shredded all the sheets with his razor-sharp teeth. the teacher told him to go home and never come back. Fangs was so sad he rewrote it by hand.
Then the next morning gave it to the teacher.

Ruairidh Smith (11)
Elrick Primary School, Westhill

Heskyball Vs Jujujaja

Five years ago there was a huge monster called Heskyball. He looked amazing. He shot footballs if other things came close. His enemy was Jujujaja. So Heskyball lived in Heskyball, the middle of the city. But once a year Jujujaja came to the city and fought Heskyball. Whoever won controlled the city. So Heskyball trained for his big match...

The match is today at 9.30am. It's the 24th of December. The match ends on the 25th of December - on Christmas day. He will hopefully win.

Mason Philip Davies (9)
Elrick Primary School, Westhill

Badstraw

My name is Kirsty. I am not the most popular girl in school, I have warts on my face and they never go, no matter how much medicine I use. Everybody teases me about them and I have no friends.

One day I went into the woods just outside school because I was so upset. I got hungry. I found a strawberry plant and had some, then I looked at my hand... I had turned into a strawberry thing and my warts had turned into seeds. After that, life got better because I could fly. I was known as Badstraw.

Sophie Tait (11)
Elrick Primary School, Westhill

The Fight For A Home!

Long ago there was a poor monster called Stinky Scott. He lived under a bridge. There was a very rich man in town called King Joey, the richest man in town. Stinky Scott would never get a home because he was stinky.

One day Scott decided to have a shower and clean himself, but he cleaned himself in a swamp so he was still stinky.

He went to someone's house. They were so kind, they let him have a shower. He felt clean. He then went to buy a new house, not any old house, a mansion.

Kyle Stevenson (9)
Elrick Primary School, Westhill

Naughty Chucky

One day in the streets of New York there was a creature called Chucky. He was cute, short and chubby. He loved getting up to mischief.
One day Chucky went to M&M World. He caused lots of mischief. He started by tipping all the M&Ms out of the tubs. Then he changed the prices of everything. After, he ate all the M&Ms. He got caught. The police came for Chucky, but he just did what he always did, he popped out his puppy eyes and the police fainted. After, he made a run for it!

Kayla Maya Brodziak (9)
Elrick Primary School, Westhill

Fireo And The Ice Rink Plot!

Fireo flew down from Planet Magmalava to Earth by using a fire powered rocket. Fireo is a spiky monster that can ice skate, but he wants to be the best, that's why he flew down to Earth. Fiero thought of a plan. He was going to melt all the ice rinks in the world! First he went to Great Britain and melted all the ice rinks with his hot, red laser beams on the end of his tail. Then he went to America and melted all the ice rinks there. Then he flew back to Magmalava to celebrate his plot.

Emma Stuart (9)

Elrick Primary School, Westhill

The Story Of The One-Eyed Demon

This is the one-eyed demon, he has wings that shoot lasers and breathes fire and can turn invisible. Life was good until one day the other demons kicked him out of hell, so he had to try and hide. Then he thought of teaming up with angels and destroying hell so he flew up and asked the angels to team up and destroy hell so they flew back down and went down to hell. They had to hide so they didn't get caught, they walked until they found a nuke so they put it on and they flew up.

Calum Thomson (10)
Elrick Primary School, Westhill

Slime Bob Eats!

When Slime Bob was going in and out of cracks like he usually does, he stumbled on his biggest nightmare... The apple house. He was already in the house because of the crack in the floor, he went into the house and he was cornered! He had no way out, he would die from the apples. Slime Bob licked the wall of concrete and said bye to the world when suddenly, he realised the wall had dissolved from his spit! So he took a big bite out of the wall and he was free! He had a superpower!

Nathan Mbaeru (10)
Elrick Primary School, Westhill

Flexy And Yeflix

It was a dark and stormy night in the streets of Hawaii, Flexy found her long lost enemy, Yeflix. She walked along behind him in the dim light and saw something in his hand. As she got closer to him she saw he had the secret fliles. She used her sticky pads to climb up his trouser leg. She sneaked into his bag and got them safely. She hurried down his trouser leg and ran quickly into the shadows. When he was out of view she ran out of the shadows, out onto the slippy, slimy path.

Lauren Hay (10)
Elrick Primary School, Westhill

Banana Fangs

Banana Fangs was a young banana hero who was almost invincible but this one time he almost got killed by Apple Core and his army. The war went on and on. They fought to the death. Then Yeflix came and threw a log at Banana Fangs but he just caught it and threw it back at him. Banana Fangs threw a banana peel at Apple Core and he slipped on it and made a hole in the ground. Cars and buildings were getting blown up. Then he got arrested for all the crimes he committed. He went to jail.

Louie James Goldie (10)
Elrick Primary School, Westhill

Blobby Goes To Earth

It was a normal day, Blobby was walking down the street when he heard a bang behind him,. He turned round and saw it was Sid, his enemy. Sid grabbed Blobby and ran to his spaceship. After a long time of flying Sid dropped Blobby out of the ship. Blobby landed with a jiggle, he was in a strange place. Then a little boy came up to him and smiled, the boy laughed and took Blobby home. Blobby showed the boy how he could shape-shift. 'I really like it here,' said Blobby.

Alisha Louise Allan (10)
Elrick Primary School, Westhill

Mr Half Man

Once upon a time there lived a man called Mr Half Man. He had red lasers as his weapons.
A few hours later he found a giant. The giant had five eyes and a big body.
A few months later they became friends. They were walking down the street and they came across a hairy monster, but he was a bad monster. The monster was called Gladiator and Half Man attacked the monster with the lasers. The monster became invisible and everyone was safe. Gladiator and Half Man won again.

Finlay Bain (9)
Elrick Primary School, Westhill

The Rainbow Disaster

My name is Rainbowglow and I have an interesting story to tell. One day when I was doing my daily walk across the rainbow I saw a horrible thing, there was a crack on the other end of the rainbow! As I got closer and closer, I got more scared by the minute, so I ran in the opposite direction but fell off the rainbow, just me, not the rainbow. And when I was falling a sweet fell into my mouth, but not any ordinary sweet, one that could make me glow in the dark.

Freya McCabe (10)
Elrick Primary School, Westhill

The Monster

There was a monster called Four Arms and he was sleeping in his den, when he heard a noise that woke him up. It was Small Ear Monster. Then Small Ear Monster got closer and closer, then he caught him in a net and he could not get out. It was bad. He got taken to a zoo. Then he was never seen for a few weeks. Then he cut open the bars one night and went far away from the base. He ran away and never was seen again for a long time. He lived in Spain.

Kieran Hunter (10)
Elrick Primary School, Westhill

Creature Friends

My creature is called Fire Head. He is good at lots of things like roasting marshmallows on his head. He is also good at skipping.

One day some people were camping where Fire Head lived, so he wanted to be friends but the people were scared of him. But then the fire went out, all they could see was Fire Head, they were all so scared. But Fire Head can put the fire out with his head. They all became best friends forever.

Kendel Laing (10)
Elrick Primary School, Westhill

The Banana Fight

He sat on his bed. Comidomie had the worst day ever. He didn't get the role of Bob the Builder. Then he had it, he would remake it himself. He hated bananas but he had to use them. First scene was when he used his banana to fix his house. That did not end well. He fought it, he punched, kicked and squashed it, squished to death. But then he remembered he hated peaches, so he carried on with Bob the Builder.

Cara Brown (9)
Elrick Primary School, Westhill

Neon Slug

The war against Planet Neon and Planet Red came again. Neon Slug had enough, so he did what he had to do, fight back. So he went to his airship and went to Planet Red.

When he got there he had to turn into a red knight. When Neon Slug got into the throne room, he trapped the king and threw the king into lava and the war was over. Neon Slug was the king of Neon Planet and threw a huge party.

Dylan James Young (9)
Elrick Primary School, Westhill

Crazy Villain And Basherbomb

In the dark alley there was a villain called Crazy Villain. He was good at every skill and trick because he was the best villain in the world. His enemies were Basherbomb and Crazy Sarah. The crazy villain went into a fight with Basherbomb, but after the fight they were friends because they teamed up against Crazy Sarah. They made the best team ever. They were best friends in the end.

Ellis Glennie (9)

Elrick Primary School, Westhill

The Adventure In Switzersweat

One nice and sunny day, an alien called Toby decided to take a holiday. *But where?* he wondered, 'Ha!' he shouted, 'I'll go to Switzersweat!' So off he went on a plane. Toby finally arrived, and wandered the streets, when suddenly he heard *Stomp! Stomp! Stomp! Stomp!* It was the sweaty guards roaming the streets. Toby froze like a statue. He was worried in case he got taken to the prison. However, he was. The guard said it was because of his ugliness. Suddenly he heard a *zzzz*, and he got rescued by the villagers in the street.

Marnie Grace Williams (10)
Glendelvine Primary School, Perth

M&M Adventure!

I embarked on my adventure, grass
towering over me like huge towers! It was already
getting dark. I'd just realised I wasn't trudging
through the forest... I was in a tiny cage in a
gloomy room. I could escape easily, so I morphed
into a rainbow and slipped through the bars. But it
wasn't that easy! Spiders came at me. Using my
rainbow laser flash I knocked them out, but a voice
came out of the blue saying, 'M&M, long time no
see.'
I recognised it, it was CB. 'CB,' I said, 'you can't do
this, we can be friends!'

Rosalie Thirsk (9)
Glendelvine Primary School, Perth

The Adventure Of Slicker

Slicker was on Negarania playing, when suddenly a meteorite crashed into the planet! Slicker was flung off his home planet onto Earth.
Slicker did not know how to get home, he looked up to where his home should be. He thought he wouldn't get home. So he had a little walk. He spotted something moving. It was a security camera and it had spotted him! Suddenly a few police cars came up and some policemen chased Slicker into an alleyway but Slicker shape-shifted into a bat and darted between the police, he flew off into the night sky and home.

Joel Hepburn (9)
Glendelvine Primary School, Perth

Fluffy Makes Friends

Fluffy is on Earth scaring people. He stops to have a rest and he has a think. He realises he hasn't been very nice. So Fluffy wants to make friends. So he throws his sword away! Then he sees someone, so Fluffy says, 'Hello!' Now he has made a few friends already! But he has to go back to Saturn. So he says, 'Goodbye,' gets into his spaceship and flies into the blue sky. He is very happy. He lets people visit him. So he has people to speak to. Sometimes Fluffy goes down to Planet Earth to say hello!

Eve Errington-Goulty (8)
Glendelvine Primary School, Perth

Untitled

I'm Topsyturvy, I'm from the sun. Ouch. I fell off the sun. I'm lost in a city on Planet Earth, I'm so scared. Humans don't like me. They run away. I try to make friends but everyone runs away. What's this? It looks like a spaceship with a point. Just then a boy comes up and says it's a rocket. It goes into space. Just then we have an idea, I will fly home. I ask for a ride but Dooglies try to stop us, but the boy stops the Dooglies and I fly to the sun with the boy.

Megan Berry (8)
Glendelvine Primary School, Perth

The Smile

One day Smile's planet, Cuddlemonkey, was about to blow up! So he got into his rocket, started the engine and flew to Earth. It was dark but he saw a place to live. He walked up. He shivered. It was cold. He saw a light in a room so he walked in. There was a little girl. 'Argh, Mumma, Pappa, come quickly, something is in my room.'
They came quickly and started to smile. They said, 'Aww, he is cute! We can keep him!' And so they did.

Eilidh Williamson (10)
Glendelvine Primary School, Perth

Tom And Jim Lost On Planet Zorg

Jim and I are lost on Planet Zorg and we can't find our way home. 'Where do we go? I think we should go and ask some villagers for help.' So I told Jim and her eight eyes and we set off to find some villagers, but nobody had heard of Cloud Cuckoo Land. We did not know how to get home. We went to their teleporter and it did not have Cloud Cuckoo Land so I guessed we were lost...

Innes Murdo Liddle (9)

Glendelvine Primary School, Perth

The Bug Fight

Darkness, yet again Betty Bed Bug was underneath someone's bed. Silence, were they asleep? Carefully Betty climbed up the back of the bed frame and peered over the top. Yes they were. Betty pulled herself on top of the bed frame and flew down slowly. She crawled over to her next victim. She took out her claws... then suddenly something knocked her off the bed. Daisy Dreamer! Daisy Dreamer was the only person that could beat Betty. She kicked her and threw her out of the window. All the bugs cheered and Betty Bed Bug was never seen again!

Cerys Goodall (11)

Portessie Primary School, Buckie

The Story Of Parkour

One day a guy called Parkairey loved Parkour, but his mum didn't allow it. But that night there was a bright light and it took him to another planet, he never knew where he was at. He saw his enemy Dr Evil Porkchop. So Parkairey had a plan to hide from him, because he didn't want to stay there forever. The plan was to try to become friends with him. He went out and found him. Dr Evil was mean to him. So he asked him. Dr Evil said, 'Only if you become friends with my friends.'
Parkairey said, 'Okay.'

Joe Murray (10)
Portessie Primary School, Buckie

Puffybogleye Strikes

One day in a forest, a family were on a walk in the summer. As they were walking they heard a strange sound. A a great, big black cloud swooped over in front of them. It said, 'My name is Puffybogleye and I have come to rule the world.' He threw a snowball at them and then they started to run away but one of the big brothers stayed behind and Puffybogleye stole him and flew away. Puffybogleye flew to the black rock and tried to make the brother Puffybogleye's sidekick so they could rule the world together.

Catie Carter (11)
Portessie Primary School, Buckie

Untitled

Mr Homework Eater is very strict and sly. He hides in the shadows. He has five legs, four arms. He loves to eat Maths homework and ice cream. He likes the number 99. He has one hobby and that is paper mâché. Then one day he got told that he would get to go on vacation because he'd made the best paper mâché in the world. So he got a medal, then he went back home and showed everyone in the town. Then after, everyone loved him so much, he stayed out in the light forever.

Jasmine Castel (9)
Portessie Primary School, Buckie

Fish Face Goes To Earth

Fish Face likes to go to Earth to catch fish. He picks their eyes out and eats them with tomato sauce. But Squiggly Octo steals his fish eyes. Once Squiggly Octo stole his fish eyes, so Fish Face dived into the water to get them back, but the bad thing is he can't swim. So he starts to drown. Then Squiggly Octo sees that he is drowning so Squiggly Octo helps him get up to the surface and gives him his fish back and then they make up and Fish Face goes back to his planet to tell his friends.

Isla Coull (11)

Portessie Primary School, Buckie

Electric Shock Back Flip

One gloomy, rainy day, Lightning Execute was walking through the park. It was going great until he met Sunshine. The look on his dark blue face said it all. He was absolutely furious! He was so mad that he accidentally slipped on a big, yellow banana peel, did a back flip and gave Sunshine an electric shock. Then he blamed her for leaving the banana peel there. He was so mad he threatened to do it again! Sunshine ran away, and that's how Lightning Execute can now do an electric shock back flip.

Eden Wojcik (10)
Portessie Primary School, Buckie

Spike Girl In Spike Land

One day Spike Girl saw a nice person and she hated nice people, so she got ready to run. Ready, steady and go and away she went to fight the nice person. She used all she had. She used her spikes on her head, she used her really, really sharp teeth and her sharp claws. It took ages for her to kill the weird, nice person. It took five hours. After all that she went out with her boyfriend. She was not the only one that liked spikes. They went out for dinner. They had fish and chips and pizza.

Courtney Grant (10)

Portessie Primary School, Buckie

All About Chomp

Sir Flying Chomp is a bug-like creature. He hates humans. He also jumps into your dreams. When the dog gets the blame for eating the cat's food it is actually Chomp! Sometimes at night he jumps into the children's dreams. When he jumps into the dreams he can make them really funny.
One night Chomp jumped into a dream and made it funny by going to a slime park. Also when he eats, he can eat as much as he wants and not get full! If a child saw Chomp they would scream!

Regan Duncan (11)
Portessie Primary School, Buckie

Zappy's Flight

As Zappy flew about on his thunder cloud, suddenly he started to get hungry. He flew down and zapped a cow and had a great lunch. So he jumped back on his cloud and flew to Neptune to see his brother Zam. On his way to Earth he met an alien with four arms and a blaster. Zappy shot a lightning bolt and Zam was turned to ashes. Zappy flew to Earth when suddenly he saw a hurricane. He was swept up and he went flying everywhere. Then he was zapped and never the same again.

Marcus Wilson (11)
Portessie Primary School, Buckie

Dat-Boi And The Green Jelly Beanstalk!

Dat-Boi went to buy a unicycle at the Zerg shop. So he did. But he got attacked by a Fazman. Luckily he got away and went home. He threw his unicycle at a bunch of Fazmen. Then Dat-Boi planted some majestical green jelly beans. A green jelly beanstalk grew out of the ground. He climbed up it and had a face off with the Dat Boi king. He threw his unicycle at the king and the king died. Dat-Boi went back down the jelly beanstalk and went home.

Archie Chalmers (10)

Portessie Primary School, Buckie

Fire Fang Becomes Santa

On the night of Christmas Eve, Fire Fang was walking along the Hawaiian beach when Santa Claus came running past her. 'Could you come and help me?' asked Santa. Fire Fang nodded her head and followed Santa. Once they were above a volcano, Santa jumped out of the sleigh into the volcano. Fire Fang didn't know what to do so she delivered all the presents and made all the children happy on Christmas Day and became the new Santa Claus.

Amy Imlach (10)

Portessie Primary School, Buckie

Green Giant

Green Giant was walking when he saw peas. He said, 'Peas, leave now or I'll yell Green Giant.' Oops, he shouted Green Giant. It was so loud he dropped his sweetcorn and the peas took his corn and left. 'Noooo.' His sweetcorn, his most important thing ever. He ran and ran and ran until he found a sweetcorn shop. He searched for the biggest tin there. The thing was, he did not have money so he had to steal it!

Jude Addison (11)
Portessie Primary School, Buckie

Muddled-Up Max!

Do not open your eyes as there may be a mess, because Muddled-Up Max hates perfect. If anything's perfect it will not be soon. So be aware as he will be there! He will muddle up your cupboards and all your rooms. He will trash your drawers and your bed, so when you sleep you will hurt your head. So when you see you will not believe it. When you leave he will come, you will not laugh because Muddled-Up Max is not done!

Freya Grant (10)
Portessie Primary School, Buckie

Mr Spikey The Football Player

Mr Spikey is a football player. He comes from Brazil and he plays in the World Cup. Mr Spikey has got five legs and is amazing in goal. He can save all the goals. Mr Spikey has got four eyes, he can see all around. The only thing about Mr Spikey is he bursts lots of balls.

Logan Wood (10)
Portessie Primary School, Buckie

Storm

Storm was flying majestically through the cold sky when Lord Slither-Snake came up from the sky. Storm used his lightning sword to slash Lord Slither-Snake, but then Lord Slither-Snake bit Storm and he fell all the way. His pet cloud, AIR (artificial intelligence robot) came to save him and Storm landed softly on AIR. Suddenly Lord Slither-Snake came and chomped on AIR. Storm was feeling extremely furious and sad at the same time. He was so mad he turned into a stormy, dark and rainy cloud, he threw his lightning crown away and zapped Lord Slither-Snake... RIP AIR.

Leo Tonsic (11)
Portlethen Primary School, Aberdeen

Yartly's Adventure

Yartly was stomping along the street. Yartly had colossal feet, huge eyes, really uneven skin, huge feet, enormous hands. Yartly was used to the heat, he plodded along the street. Yartly started to plod down the street to the park, where he stumbled across an unusual person. His name was Mr Gag. He was a nice person. He said to Yartly, 'What are you doing here crazy Yartly?'

'I'm just a bit lost Mr Gag. I'm really sorry Mr Gag, can I stay?'

'No,' he said. So Yartly went for a look, saw a zeppelin and didn't go on it.

Fraser Haydn Cardno (10)

Portlethen Primary School, Aberdeen

The Cliffhanger

Below the deepest part of the cliff, there was a ferocious creature named Tsunami. His coat was blue and he had a dangerous water sprayer with water venom.

One day Tsunami went to the deepest part of the ocean ever, Tsunami glided as quick as lightning to the Lords of Fire. Helena, head of the Lords, had no idea about the danger that was coming for them. However Tsunami was spotted by the humans, who shrieked in terror. 'Tsunami come, come to the humans, come now,' snarled Tsunami, he was calling for a tsunami. Danger was coming for them!

Julia Bugdal (10)
Portlethen Primary School, Aberdeen

Dibo

Dibo was flying in and out of trees with his super powerful, colossal wings majestically. All of a sudden, Dibo spotted some explorers with guns. Dibo was petrified but he was not looking where he was going and as loud as thunder he hit a tree and fell to the ground... The explorers heard, so they came over with guns in hand. Dibo had to do something before he died. He thought he could use his fire breath attack to burn the explorers. He did just that and the explorers were shooting Dibo. As fast as a jet, Dibo escaped.

Luke Robert Scotson (10)
Portlethen Primary School, Aberdeen

The Nestle Adventure

Suddenly, Fluff fell down the trench. Fluff used her claws to keep hold. The poor Nestle had been dented, but it was surprisingly still OK. It climbed up. 'Phew,' the poor creature climbed up a mountain and found its dream, since it was a baby. Food. She ran and ran and saw fish, steak and loads more. Eating all she could with her sharp teeth, again she lost grip of the mountain and fell, jagging the edges of the trench. Getting a grip, using her supersonic speed to speed up, she then grabbed all she could carry and teleported home.

Arran Coull (10)
Portlethen Primary School, Aberdeen

The Demented Giraffe

Farty was a big and clumsy, demented giraffe. He had a very long neck and even longer legs, with a very silky skin which was covered with spikes all over. He had two very big eyes. He lived under the water in a shipwreck, but he was stuck... Farty was stuck under a water cave with no food and nothing to do, he had to break out. He thought for a while, how could he break out? 'Oh yeah,' he muttered to himself, 'I can use my fart rockets to break out.' *Faaaaaart* went his rockets, he had broken out...

Ethan John Saum (10)
Portlethen Primary School, Aberdeen

Blob's Adventure

Desperate for heat in the darkest, coldest night, Blob used his sixteen headlight eyes to light up the night. When suddenly he saw a cave, so Blob used his razor-sharp claws to dig into the freezing snow to climb up the steep mountain. Blob finally got into the cave and sat down to rest, when suddenly a huge rainbow came and said, 'Hello,' to Blob. Then he found a colossal rocket ship so Blob went in it. With a huge *bang!* the colossal rocket took off. Blob was panic-stricken. Blob tried to calm down when he landed...

Mia Louise Donald (10)
Portlethen Primary School, Aberdeen

Quackers Goes Mad!

Once upon a time, there was a small duck who loved long waddles in the park. Waiting for someone to come and feed him, he noticed someone else feeding a peculiar creature. It had sharp claws, pointy teeth, dark red eyes and dark black wings. At the sight of the creature anyone would flinch.

Weeks went by and he still didn't have the courage to go and get food. Then one day he did. He knew what he had to, he was starving. *Smash*, *bang*, the creature attacked him. He was knocked out in a flash. Now Quackers was mad.

Grant Lindsay (10)

Portlethen Primary School, Aberdeen

The Lost Unigirl

Uni, the Unigirl, was lost. She was surrounded by tall green things. Uni started to gallop around. As she was galloping around she saw something up high in the air so she used her sharp claws to climb up the tall, green things. Then she saw someone, she climbed over and asked the girl, 'Hi, my name is Uni, I'm a Unigirl and I have two questions to ask. Where am I and how do I get back to my habitat, Plodo?'

'Well, my name is Lily and you are in a jungle I'm afraid to say, not Plodo...'

Holly McPherson (10)

Portlethen Primary School, Aberdeen

Evil Blobby, Good Blobby

Once upon a time a girl found this sharp blob with a beaver tail. It looked upset, but why? She decided to take it home. Every night she heard laughing voices, but what was it? Finally, one night, she woke up, she saw her purple blob was red. The blob, whilst being red, had fierce teeth and fiercely amazing eyes. She got scared. It moved slowly like it was not harmful, but tried to attack. The blob said, 'My name is Blobby, I turn evil when I'm angry, I can't get home.' The blob got taken back to the pond.

Kornelia Bartnicka (10)

Portlethen Primary School, Aberdeen

Tom The Bogeyman

One day there was a cheerless, colossal man called Tom the Bogeyman. He ate bogies every single day. Tom met a girl and he liked her, but the girl said, 'You are repulsive and monstrous, I hate you.' Tom felt melancholic and went home. Tom began to stop eating bogies so he could get the girl. Tom had to do a gruesome quest, which was to get a ghastly sword that you had to get or else you wouldn't win the girl. He had to go to the abandoned warehouse, he saw it and clutched it, and got the girl.

Taylor Jane Stephen (10)

Portlethen Primary School, Aberdeen

The Bogey Monster

Bogey was having a normal day on the moon, but then there was a hurricane and he fell off the moon and fell on Liam. Liam was the bogeyman. When Bogey fell on Liam, he turned into the bogeyman. He started to get really hungry. He ate Bogey and started to eat his bogies, but he was still hungry. He started to go around the town hypnotising people with the swirls on his head. When he hypnotised the people, they followed him to the moon, but he ate one person and he was full. He transformed into his normal self.

Olivia Jackson (10)
Portlethen Primary School, Aberdeen

Untitled

Aaron was running on ten tiny legs, he fell and scanned the amazing desert with his five eyes. He saw an eagle. The eagle was terrifyingly hungry and flapping like wind. Aaron ran. The eagle caught him. Soon they were at the top of a large nest in a massive tree. Aaron was a red creature. The eagle loved the colour red so he stole him. Aaron tried to climb down. He saw the eagle was coming for him. His robot-like arms climbed faster. It was no use, the eagle caught him. He flew to a volcano and dropped him.

Liam Macarthur (10)

Portlethen Primary School, Aberdeen

Untitled

Suddenly, Elppin woke up and he was in the sea. As quick as a flash, Elppin was trying to get up to the top of the choppy sea. Although he was a dustbin monster, he could still swim as well as a fish. He needed to get back to the dustbin. Unless he found a marvellous dustbin just right for him. Although everything was soaking, he found a dustbin all rusty, but when he tried to fit in, he couldn't because of his huge hands. He squeezed his bus-sized eye in. Elppin slithered along with his snail back.

Kai Watson (10)
Portlethen Primary School, Aberdeen

The Vampire

In the ocean there was a creature, she was a vampire mermaid called Holly. She was queen of all vampire mermaids. Her father's name was Luke. One day Holly went to prank her sister. Mia was second queen, she was very jealous of her sister and she was not as beautiful either. Holly was the beautiful one. Luke, Holly and Mia's father, always told them to get along with each other. But it didn't work, they just wouldn't stop arguing. They never got on, even when they were babies.

Megan Mary Farley (10)
Portlethen Primary School, Aberdeen

Untitled

One day a big monster came to New York called Godzilla. He smashed the city into pieces of rubble. He used his wolverine claws to smash the Statue of Liberty, then he went to London. He smashed Big Ben with his heat vision then he went to Paris and kicked the Eiffel Tower. Then he went to Egypt and he used his heat breath to burn the pyramids. Then he went back to London and stomped on Buckingham Palace. Then the military got a nuke and dropped it on him. He ran back to the ocean and went deep down.

Kieran Strachan (10)
Portlethen Primary School, Aberdeen

The Mysterious Creature

Although Snowy was struggling to climb up the steep, snow-packed mountain, Snowy had forgotten she had night vision eyes and super strength. She had to use them or she would fall off the mountain. She finally got up and there were three kids up at the top and they were called Josie, Heather and Kornelia. They screamed, but that was because Snowy looked terrifying. She was white and fluffy and she had four eyes, but as soon as she put on the puppy eyes they stopped and started to whisper...

Heather Lloyd (10)
Portlethen Primary School, Aberdeen

Revenge

'Hey Lil.'

'What?'

'Whatcha doing?'

'Why?'

'Because we're in a forest.'

Lily was an evilhorn. Because she's nice she was re-growing a flower.

'Why are you such a goody two shoes, re-growing flowers?' said Growls, then all of Lily's hard work was destroyed by Growls. 'Ha, ha.'

A few years later...

'Ha good one Steve, ha, ha, OK bye!' Then she remembered revenge was needed. 'Growls!' shouted Lily. In the end she got revenge. Finally she said bye and sent him to exile. She felt bad, but then she remembered revenge...

Marnie Nye (8)
Viewlands Primary School, Perth

Terra-Tor Stops One Monster Planet

One day Terra-Tor was building the final bit for the tranceforfationantor to stop one monster planet. An hour later they had finished. 'Now we need to charge it up,' said Terra in his kid voice.

So half an hour later Tor said, 'Done, now let's fire this thing up.'

Terra said, 'Of course, that's what we made it for, bud.'

'I know, I'm just too excited,' said Tor. So Tor pressed the fire button and the beam zoomed past them and one monster planet turned into two monster brother planets. Terra and Tor told everyone and they all screamed, 'Hooray!'

Murray William Leckie (9)
Viewlands Primary School, Perth

The Plane Crash

As he peered through the window of the plane, Simon realised with a jolt that they were losing height. Immediately they started plummeting to almost certain death. Around the burning wreckage, the only sounds were Sarah's screams, along with the only other survivor - that crazy guy Maronzo. They neared the crash site. Suddenly from the bushes rushed a raptor. That meant something bigger... a growler. Growlers always had territorial battles with raptors. Normally growlers won, but raptors fought hard. Now the growler had spotted Maronzo, who it picked up and ate whole. Now there was the lone raptor.

Campbell Shaw (10)
Viewlands Primary School, Perth

Crazy Eyes' Story

Crazy Eyes escapes from the core by destroying a plate and making a tsunami, it crawls out of the core and makes a nest to make friends. It makes its den out of sticks, mud and logs and steals matches to make a fire. It lives near a river for water and eats whatever it can find. It's set up and the next day goes to find friends. First it wants to find a calm creature, but it sees Shapeshifter. It tries to make friends, but Shapeshifter does not agree, then he hates him. Crazy Eyes cannot find a friend.

Sam McTeague (8)
Viewlands Primary School, Perth

Not What You Expect

Our story begins with four explorers, James, Peter, Esme and Dillon, on an old wooden boat, looking for the hand octopus. People have been scouting the Earth for years for this sea monster. When they reached the middle of the red sea they saw a ginormous multicoloured octopus. James shouted, 'Pass me the binoculars!' All four ran to the side of the boat and leaned over. Dillon fell in. They gasped. Where had he gone? A few moments later Dillon appeared, riding the enormous, hairy, scary octopus. No one knows what became of them. Do you?

Francesca Mudd (9)
Viewlands Primary School, Perth

The Depths Of The Amazon Jungle

Hello, would you like to hear about my crazy creature called Spiky? Okay. My crazy creature's name is Spiky, he lives in the depths of the Amazon Jungle, his enemies are snakes. Spiky can turn invisible. Spiky is green, which means he can disguise himself as well. Spiky is called Spiky because he has spikes all over his body.

One day, he was just normally having fun until a group of snakes came up to him, so he became invisible and was able to travel away into another part of the Amazon Jungle, where he decided to stay.

Lewis Dyson (9)
Viewlands Primary School, Perth

Chuck And The Park

Chuck was walking to the park. His flame was burning and his bright red skin was gleaming in the sunlight. He had nearly got on a swing when Mr Snoodles, Chuck's worst enemy, tried to get on the swing. They trudged up to each other and started a fight! There was pushing and shoving. There was stamping and stomping and then finally Mr Snoodles gave up. Finally Chuck had the swing to himself. But Snoodles wouldn't stop picking on him. Chuck tried to ignore it, but his flame was burning and his red face had started to sweat...

Ava Stewart (9)
Viewlands Primary School, Perth

Global Warming

Hello, my name is TD and I'm a turtle dove. No, not the bird but the two animals combined. I have a long neck with feathers flowing down and a beautiful beak placed right at the tip of my glamorous face. I came from a scientist and I was created to feed the poor, starving penguins that are suffering from the effects of global warming. My strong wings let me swoop down over the ocean to catch and transfer the fish to the penguins. They all huddle together anxiously awaiting their feast and hope that it will come.

Emma Pryor (9)
Viewlands Primary School, Perth

I Love Lollipop

One day a big mouthed, flying, scary, giant lollipop was dancing, singing along with his big mouth. He danced very fast and sang very, very loud. After all his singing and dancing he was hungry and tired, but was far too excited to stand still, as he knew that tomorrow was the first day of winter and he would be meeting up with lots more frozen, singing and dancing lollipops. Winter was the best time of year to make brand new friends, even though these friends only lasted until winter was over, he always had great fun.

Ocean-Melodie McCole (8)

Viewlands Primary School, Perth

Twime's New Friend

Twime is an African creature. He lives in a desert with hardly any water in it. So he had to walk because he couldn't use time travel yet. Time travel is only meant to be used in an emergency. On his last journey to the water river he met another of his species. He was called Clockie and they walked to the river together and had a nice drink. But suddenly Clockie fell into the river that was heading right to the African city called Capetown. Twime suddenly vanished into thin air. He reappeared with Clockie in his hands.

Amelia Hutchison (9)
Viewlands Primary School, Perth

The Stink Monster

One spooky night a young boy named Simon went out into the woods to look for endangered species with parental permission. Simon was twelve years old and would like to be a zoo keeper. What he didn't get permission for, was to look for wild animals. He saw a moose. He froze. Then he turned around and fell in the mud. *Squelch!* He cleaned himself up and walked away quickly. Then he ran into a creepy, stinky, dirty monster. He caught him with his stinky hands and that was the end of Simon. He learned his lesson.

Modou Bah (8)
Viewlands Primary School, Perth

Magimon - The Magical Monster

Magimon was wandering around the lake to have a drink. Suddenly there was a big shadow coming towards him in the water. Magimon crept back just in time to see the big animal. It was a giant crocodile and Magimon had nowhere to escape. It was getting very close, so Magimon used his magic tail to get through the crocodile into the open air. The damage that had been done to the crocodile, was that he choked on the muddy water and then he fled. Then Magimon got his drink from the lake and then carried on with his day.

Alistair John MacGregor Milne (9)
Viewlands Primary School, Perth

A Day Of Peace... Kind Of

Sammy's green eyes looked at the blue sky. He snuggled in a tree, brushing his black and white fur. Then he jumped down and crawled home. Beside his forest home he played in the river. Afterwards he wrapped up in his favourite towel. He was cosy and his fur started beaming red. Next, to dry off, he turned into a fireball from his tail down to his four paws. He was so bright that he could be seen for miles. Finally, his fluffy fur cooled back down. He got to go in his soft, comfy, warm bed to sleep.

Annabel Humphrey (9)
Viewlands Primary School, Perth

The Red Monster

I heard a weird sound, I turned on my light. What a surprise I got. There was a little, red monster with yellow eyes, riding around my bedroom on the Lego truck I built before I went to bed. It crashed into my bedside cabinet and the truck broke and the Lego blocks went everywhere. There was steam coming from the monster and it ran and hid under my bed. I thought I was dreaming and went back to sleep.

In the morning I got up and I saw the smashed truck. Was it really a dream..?

Eli Thomas Barron (10)
Viewlands Primary School, Perth

The Refused King Of Latsyland

Booba walked along the beach and saw the king of Latsyland, he was very poorly and within one blink he was gone. The guards saw Booba and asked him to be the king, but he refused because he said he wanted to be with his family and walked off. The guards stopped him and told him that his family could stay with him and live with him. They took the crown off the old king and placed it on Booba's fat head and screamed, 'Everybody, here is Booba, the new king of Latsyland.'

Abbie Todd (9)
Viewlands Primary School, Perth

The Sneaky Wolik

Once upon a time there was a wolik, it was half wolf, half snake, the head of a wolf and the body of a snake. The snake's body was very long, as long as a metre stick, the colour was red, brown and black as well as the body. The wolf's black fur was glossy and the wolf's ears were tiny, bouncy balls and it was not any ordinary snake or wolf, it had legs and arms. Then it went to the market and took everything in the market and went back home very, very full.

Layan AlHamdan (8)
Viewlands Primary School, Perth

Adventure

Lord Fungus shoots laser beams at Planet Mimic. Brainiac shape-shifts into a pink flamingo. Flamingo uses hyper beam. The ship has a trick, it shoots an incredible beam. Brainiac uses a forcefield. Brainiac shoots a beam, the ship explodes.

Liam Neave (8)
Viewlands Primary School, Perth

YoungWriters
Est.1991

YOUNG WRITERS INFORMATION

We hope you have enjoyed reading this book – and that you will continue to in the coming years.

If you're a young writer who enjoys reading and creative writing, or the parent of an enthusiastic poet or story writer, do visit our website **www.youngwriters.co.uk**. Here you will find free competitions, workshops and games, as well as recommended reads, a poetry glossary and our blog.

If you would like to order further copies of this book, or any of our other titles, then please give us a call or visit **www.youngwriters.co.uk**.

Young Writers
Remus House
Coltsfoot Drive
Peterborough
PE2 9BF
(01733) 890066
info@youngwriters.co.uk